I0797816

A LITTLE GUIDE TO MEDITATION

For children who want to connect with the world

Written by Ms. Kiusam
Illustrated by Rodrigo Andrade
Translated by Sandra Tamele

TATE

First published 2024 by order of the Tate Trustees
by Tate Publishing, a division of Tate Enterprises Ltd,
Millbank, London SW1P 4RG

www.tate.org.uk

Translation by Sandra Tamele, 2023

Design: Roanne Marner
Editor: Cherise Lopes-Baker
Production: Juliette Dupire

A catalogue record for this book is available from the British Library

HB ISBN 978 1 84976 910 5
PB ISBN 978 1 84976 911 2

Distributed in the United States and Canada by ABRAMS, New York
Library of Congress Control Number applied for

Colour reproduction by DL Imaging Ltd, London
Printed and bound in China by C&C Offset Printing Co., Ltd

Ms. Kiusam

I dedicate this book to my father Ciciá, who is like a cup overflowing with emotions; and to my mother Erdi (in memoriam), who filled my life with pure light and joy.

To Érico Felix de Souza, the holistic therapist that saved my life in Espírito Santo when he realigned my chakras, planting the seed of this story in me, marking my return to São Paulo, and a new phase in my life.

I would like to thank Ranadhiira Renata, a Kemetic Yoga instructor, Ayurvedic therapist and social worker, for her generosity in training and informing us about the postures, bringing us a wealth of knowledge about Egypt, and the African continent. I am immensely grateful for the conversations and exchanges I had with Professor Ruy do Carmo Póvoas, linguist, Babalorixá of Ilê Axé Ijexá, of the Ijexá nation, where Oxum is worshipped. He brought the necessary confirmations of this great ancestor linked to Oxibatá and Meditation, through itans and myths.

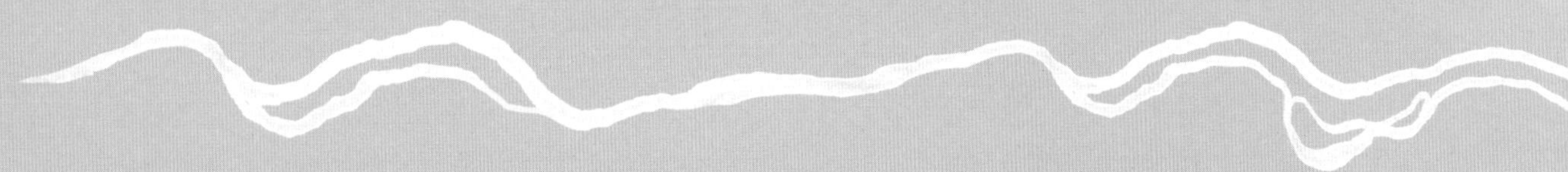

Rodrigo Andrade

I dedicate this to my father, Antonio Lucio, who was a turbulent man in the past, but is like a river of calm and welcoming waters today. Long live the king.

Come here, sit next to me.
Relax your mind and your heart,
breathe slowly.
Listen to what I'm about to tell you, as we work
to become one.
The vibrations of love are welcoming,
like watching a hummingbird
drinking nectar, or
dreaming
to the beat of a drum.
Do you know that tum, tum, tum of your heart
like the beat of the drum?
Manifesting scarlet,
vibrating to the sacred rum.

Relax with me.
Relax with me.

Rum: The biggest of the three drums
used in Afro-Brazillian religious rituals.

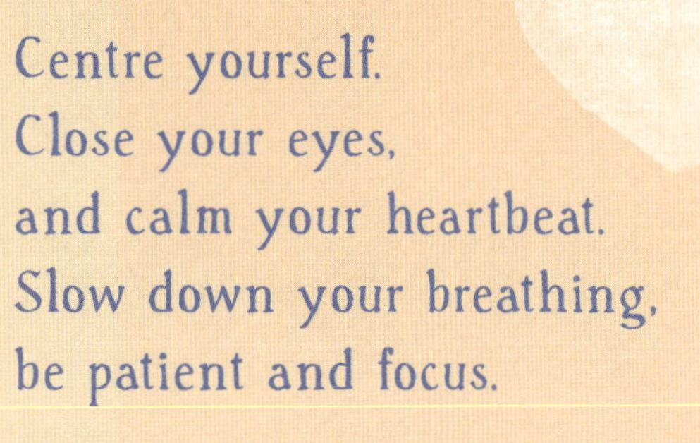

Centre yourself.
Close your eyes,
and calm your heartbeat.
Slow down your breathing,
be patient and focus.

Centre with me.
Centre with me.

Pay attention.
Breathe the wind in through your nose
and then breathe it out through your mouth.
Slowly, breathe in.
Slowly, breathe out.

Breathe with me.
Breathe with me.

Visualise and create.
As you breathe in and breathe out,
relax every part of your body.
Imagine many colours spinning
and spinning
in a never-ending kaleidoscope.

Imagine with me.
Imagine with me.

Release.
Kaleidoscopic winds come in through your head and nose,
but do not forget your hands and feet.
They turn your body into a runway,
a driving force,
connected to the universe.
They are the source
for letting yourself go,
turning you into happy,
vibrating energies.

Release with me.
Release with me.

Be aware of how
the different colours
will affect you.
Remember:
white, appeases,
violet, transforms,
indigo, purifies,
yellow, energises,
orange, regenerates,
blue, calms,
green, heals,
red, awakens.

Paint with me.
Paint with me.

Everything works out the more focused you are.
Close your eyes,
Place your hand over your heart.
Be gentle in the search for union,
breathe the wind in, and then breathe it out naturally.
With your inner eyes, forget about the time.
Soon, all those loud thoughts will quiet down
and fall into a deep sleep inside soft clouds.
With an empty Ori there is no room for confusion.
Peace is restored, bringing effusion.

Gesture with me.
Gesture with me.

Ori: Head

Be grateful.
To the universe
and planet Earth,
to mothers and fathers,
to siblings and cousins,
to grandmas and grandpas,
to aunties and uncles,
to friends and teachers,
The house you live in, and the happy memories it has.
The food that nourishes you, and party times.
Adupé! Adupé! Adupé!
Thank you! Thank you! Thank you!
Thank you! Thank you! Thank you!
For the good faith and the cuddle.

Appreciate with me.
Appreciate with me.

Don't be surprised.
At this point,
your conscience
will be cracked open.
With your eyes still closed,
you will see colours dancing.
Enjoy the moment,
and tell me about it later.

Enjoy with me.
Enjoy with me.

You will feel as if your body is
floating in the air.
As a witness,
contemplate the stars,
the moon or the sun.
Listen to the sounds
of the universe,
sharpen your hearing.
– Ommmmm!
Everything is sensational.
Focus on a big bubble,
the biggest you can imagine.
Fly, fly …
Fly closer to the bubble.
Are you there yet?

Float with me.
Float with me.

Place your hands on the bubble very gently.
Just feel the energy, and let it in.
Connect and drift outside time again.

Connect with me.
Connect with me.

Feel your little body
charged with strength, and emotion,
with the energy
that emanates from the universe.
And, with awareness,
allow it to expand,
awakening your spirit,
full of immensity.

Expand with me.
Expand with me.

And come back.
Slowly move your little fingers,
your toes, and your hands.
Flex and point your feet.
Release any tension.
Stretch until you reengage.
Move your body gently
for as long as you need.
Lastly, open your eyes
as your heart overflows with love.

Love with me.
Love with me.

Feel your heart growing bigger, and bigger.
It is love, love, love
vibrating in you so strongly.
Look around and embrace
whomever and whatever is close to you.
Let your body light up
and soon you will
say the magic word
that makes our lives fuller.

Wake up with me.
Wake up with me.

What do we call this power of communion?
I know, it can only be
gratitude.
Much more
than a simple thank you,
it is when our Self
gives thanks with compassion,
moved by reconnecting.

Give thanks with me.
Give thanks with me.

It is time for discovery.
Revelation: we are stars!
And we play, we sing, we study,
we write, we solve problems
like stars do.
Stars are respectful, and loving,
they cry,
and smile and eat treats.

Discover with me.
Discover with me.

Do you know the name
of what we just did?
I'll give you a hug in your dreams,
if you can guess it right now.
I'll give you one,
I'll give you two,
I'll give you three chances.
So just try.
Listen carefully,
I know you'll get it.

That's right;

It's an ancient philosophy
called meditation.

Learn with me.
Learn with me.

Who is the source of meditation after all?

Some are inspired by Buddha,
others prefer Krishna.

I try to solve this mystery,
but can't help but notice all the references are men.
Why is that?

Question with me.
Question with me.

I don't know where your inspiration comes from.
Mine comes from female strength. Let me teach you of her.
From the ancient foremother that walks on *otás* in fresh waters.
She washes her *idá* and smoothes her feet,
shines her *idés*,
regardless of the tides.
African queen
who casts shells and obís in divination,
enchants us with her dance moves,
and covers her body in cowrie-shells.

Come with me.
Come with me.

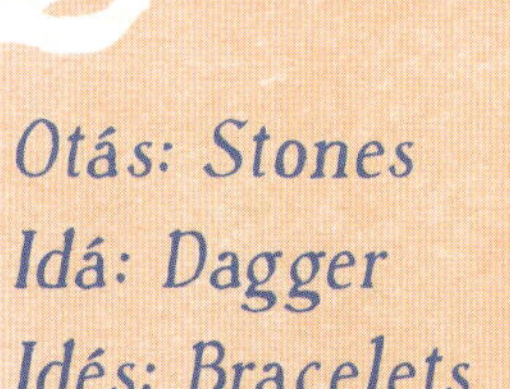

Otás: Stones
Idá: Dagger
Idés: Bracelets

A strategist, the protector of women.
Determined, she overcomes hardships.
She learnt how to empty her Ori
with the sacred leaf
called Oxibatá.
Venerated by the Great Mothers
it was given many names:
Egyptian lotus, water hyacinth,
nymphaea, water lily.
I surprise people when I say that
this leaf came from Africa.

Be inspired with me.
Be inspired with me.

Who is the female deity that inspires me to meditate, after all?
Her name is Oxum
and she only brings well-being, axé.
With Oxibatá,
she learnt to meditate
to not be anxious
and to radiate light among her loved ones.
Obatalá gave her the Blue Lotus of the Nile.
This oxibatá, the bringer of
wisdom, intelligence and empowerment,
was worshiped by Isis and Nefertum,
the Egyptian goddesses,
and loved by Ewá, Iemanjá and Oxum,
grounded by the holy iabás.

Meditate with me.
Meditate with me.

Oxibatá means "the one that will not submit";
the leaf that brings dignity in life and leads to autonomy.
Though its roots are deep in the mud, the flower stands proud,
and beautiful, releasing its perfume in the sun.
I salute and celebrate its honourable African ancestry.
I venerate women, the givers of life.
I put everything in its proper place,
with my mind and body connected and open, my roots grounded,
vibrating to the frequency of love,
our thoughts transformed.

I remember to simply feel,
look, and breathe in.
Breathe out, touch, and vibrate.
Quiet ... Feel the silence.
Remember, Love is always gentle

My name is ***Ms. Kiusam***

I wear a number of hats, but the ones I value the most are: Iyálòrìsà Kiusam de Osòssí, pedagogue, doctor in education, masters in psychology from the University of São Paulo (USP) and integrative therapist. I am also a writer of what I call the Black-Brazilian Literature of Enchantment for Children and Young Adults. I work as a trainer of education professionals on education, ethnic-racial and gender relations, with a focus on anti-racist education.

My name is ***Rodrigo Andrade***

When I was little I fell in love with libraries and picture books, I then studied graphic arts and specialised in web development. Today, I work in the field of digital education, developing multimedia content, and animations. I look for creative ways to approach playfulness and diversity in every sense of the words, and they are always there when I'm drawing. That little Black boy in the library, with his head full of images, is always there in everything that I do.